SCAM PREVENTION

SCAM PREVENTION

D. MORGAN

Contact author for more information:
347.385.4351

To order additional copies of this book, contact:
Xlibris
1-888-795-4274
www.Xlibris.com
Orders@Xlibris.com
769642

SCAM PREVENTION

D. MORGAN

Contact author for more information:
347.385.4351

To order additional copies of this book, contact:
Xlibris
1-888-795-4274
www.Xlibris.com
Orders@Xlibris.com
769642

ACKNOWLEDGEMENTS

To my lovely Mother, Josephine!,
To my Wife Shavonna!,
To my Children!,
To Mr. Gibson!
And to the whole Staff at Xlibris Corporation!

CONTENTS

INTRODUCTION

A wife and husband owned a small business called "QUICK BAKE", as a young couple, Sarah being 28 years old and Ben 32. Both worked hard to not only finance their business, but also to operate it on an everyday basis. Sarah worked as a nurse for 8 years, saving $270.000. Ben who worked as a bus driver, saved up $125.000, taking out a bank loan for $140.000 to put with Sarah's part of the money. Together, they invested $ 535.000 into their small business, building a profitable company throughout the years.

One day while Ben was home, he received a call from his bank where he took out the loan to start "QUICK BAKE". The bank informs Ben that his $140.000 loan has been increased to $300.000 and the bank was calling to make sure he'd made the request for said amount, and that it was not a fraud attempt. Alarmed, Ben immediately

tells the bank it wasn't him. The bank asks Ben for some personal information (social security number, date of birth and etc. . .) to verify it's him and cancel the increasement. Ben gives the banker the requested information. After the bank verifies it's him, they assure him everything's been taken care of. Ben thanks the banker and goes about his day.

About a month later, Sarah uses a company credit card and it's declined. Sarah call's her credit card company, and they explain to her that her card is maxed out. She hangs up the phone and calls ben, he assures her that he didn't use the card and it must be a mistake. The couple soon finds out, it wasn't a mistake, but their identity has been stolen. Not only have their company accounts been wiped out, but also their personal account as well.

I'm sure by now, you know that the call Ben received over a month ago about the increasement in his loan, wasn't a banker or a bank company, but an identity thieve. Also known as a scammer. But how was he able to do so much with just one call? Even get into Sarah's account! As complicated as it sounds, it's simple.

There are many way's the scammer could have found out about bens loan. The scammer could have gotten the bill out of their mailbox, worked for the loan company, been a close friend who knew about the loan or gotten a list of public records on small businesses. But even so, how did the scammer get into Sarah's account? Ben didn't give Sarah's information. Once Ben gave his personal information, anyone Ben ever had an account with, now can also be victimized. This depends on the scammer's level of expertise

THREE TYPE OF SCAMMERS

BEGINNERS LEVEL OF SCAMMING

On this level, the scammer might call all the banks that are widely known and has an automated system, using it until they hit the jackpot. Most bank automated systems allow you to look up your account using your social security number (ss#) if you don't have the account number on hand. When an account is found, the scammer can request a new card to a new address.

MID-LEVEL OF SCAMMING

A notch above the beginner, this level of scam would do something similar as the first level, but instead of ordering new card, the scammer would order a replacement card to your address already on file. The reason for this, is because a replacement card is given when you a damage

your card and allows the scammer to use your card while you use it too! This is because nothing is changed on the card, and the bank doesn't ask to many security questions.

Also the card is delivered to your address, which doesn't cause any red flags. I know what you're thinking! If the scammer orders the card to my house, how would they get it? The scammer would order It overnight with UPS or FED EX and take the chance of catching the parcel service before they get to your door! Meaning the scammer was somewhere by your house! Scary huh.

PRO LEVEL OF SCAMMING

This level has no limit, and a person on this level will not do any of the above things mentioned in the first two level's, except ship the card to your address, but most likely just open a P.O. Box in your name. The first thing a scammer will do on this level is a public record check on their victim. Many online websites offer personal information for a cheap cost. These sites provide full names, your children names, spouse name, parents name, date of birth's (DOB), current and previous addresses, and names of people you have lived with, within the past 10 years. Get this! It's all legal! After a scammer gets this information on you. The next step is to request a credit

report on you. And we all know what a credit report has on it! As you can see, Ben and Sarah were dealing with a Pro scammer, and the scammer most likely got Sarah's SS# from a bank she shared with Ben.

I will take you through real life steps, so that you can prevent scam and not end up like Ben and Sarah. Because even though most identity theft victims receive their money back, fixing your credit back can lead to many years of stress.

BACKGROUND

First, here's a little info on credit cards, debit cards and Checks.

HOW CREDIT CARDS CAME ABOUT:

The use of credit cards began after the Second World War, and their use has skyrocketed in the past 10 years. There are currently over 1 billion MasterCard and visa cards in use, plus countless gas, phone and store cards for everything, including rent and groceries.

The concept of the credit card is based on the precept of purchasing credit. Store owners used to offer credit to a select few of their customers. They allowed them to purchase now and pay either at the end of the month or beginning of the month. Primarily larger stores that have several branches further developed the idea.

HOW DO CREDIT CARDS WORK:

Credit cards are obtained from an issuing institution or bank that the consumer deals with directly. When making a purchase, the merchant receives the card that bears the name, account number and signature of the buyer. The merchant then inserts the card in to a card-reading machine (Black Box) and enters the amount of the purchase. The buyer or bearer of the card would sign the appropriate form. The merchant is the to verify the signature against the one on the card. Occasionally, the merchant are obligated to call and verify that the person has sufficient credit and/or available funds (this never happens). At the end of this procedure, the merchant gives the goods and a copy of the signed form to the buyer. The merchant retains a copy and sends it to the institution issuing the card to receive the payment.

There are several type of credit cards, but they can principally be divided into two categories: Store cards and General Cards!

The first type, store credit cards are those that can only be used at specific stores or their branches throughout the country or world, such as SEARS or JC PENNY's store cards.

The second and by far more popular, and are the general credit cards that have more of an international nature and can be used anywhere. The cardholder may withdraw cash or purchase goods or services and then reimburse the company by making minimum monthly installments as determined by the issuing institution. The issuing institution receives an interest on the remaining balance ranging from 18% and more annually. Cards such as American express, MasterCard, Visa, Discover, carte blanche, diner card and etc. .., fall into this category.

DEBIT CARDS:

Debit and withdrawal cards-also known as bankcards, ATM cards and check cards. Theses allow the cardholder to withdraw cash against his/her account to cover the value.

A debit card is a convenient alternative to cash and checks. "Debit" means "subtract" and when you use the card, you are subtracting money from your deposit account, such as a checking account. There will be no monthly bill, because the purchase amount is automatically deducted from your checking or current account. They are your best choice for a bankcard.

CHECKS:

Regular checks are issued by an individual against a personal account within a financial institution. These type of checks are described as a written document according to agree upon formalities for exchange and party liquidation. It includes an order issued by a (the payer) to another (the financial institution) to pay a third party or whomever the later specifies (the payee), as specific.

Now that we have covered some basic things about cards and checks, let's get down to prevention.

Remember, that when most of us think of someone stealing our identity, we visualize a con who's hardcore and dumb. Please remove this from your mind now! Scammers are smart and professional, very articulate in speech, presentable in attire and again, smart and professional.

Out of 100 people, maybe 5 of them check their credit report every year and this isn't even enough. Identity theft is at an all-time high, so thieves are able to get account numbers, SS#'s and passwords. The first step to scam prevention is being protective over your SS#.

SS# (SOCIAL SECURITY NUMBER)

Your ss# is the key to the vault, without it, Scammers can't access your full identity. Understand that a pro scammer can access your accounts with just the last 4 digits of your ss# and with those last 4 digit's, gain your full ss#.

For instant, there are credit reporting agencies who only require those last 4 of your ss# and when a scammer gains access to your full credit report, the report will show your full ss# under personal information.

This is why it's never safe to give your ss# over the phone, email or mail. Believe it or not, most ss#s are stolen from doctor office's, tax offices, insurance offices and get this one, your cable company! My cable company? yes, your cable company. Here's how! Let's go back to Sarah and Ben story, now just inmaging the same scammer who got ben to give up his personal information, called your local cable company and pretended they worked for that same cable company, but in a different department. Pretended to have you on the phone with them, changing your ss#?

CABLE COMPANY EXAMPLE:

"Hello, thank you for calling NY Cable, how can i help you today? "Said the cable operator.

"Hello, my name is con from the fraud department of NY Cable" replied the scammer.

"Hey con, I'm Tim, how can i help you"

"I have a customer on the other side of the line. Seems that the customer used their tax ID number when setting up this account by mistake. The customers phone number on file is 517-001-0100 so you can pull up the account on your end" said the scammer.

"Okay con, i have that account in front of me, that's for James Moore? "Asked the cable operator

"Yes, that's correct Tim, I'm going to transfer the customer over to you now. I fixed his ss# and he wants to upgrade his cable package" said the scammer.

"No problem con, you can transfer the customer over. I'll be more than happy to help him" replied the cable operator." Thank you Tim, before i transfer the customer, can you verify the ss# you have on your side. Just to make sure, its reflecting correctly on your end." said the scammer.

"No problem, it's 980-00-0102, is that correct"

"Yes, thank you Tim" the scammer said, disconnecting the call.

Do i need to continue, the scammer was able to get someone's whole SS# using a phone number and good speech. I know you're saying to yourself, how can i stop this type of scamming?, well, good thing you bought this book.

The first thing you do to combat this type of scam is don't list your number in any phone books or online. Privacy is a right. Also, putting a password on your account's will make it more difficult for a scammer to penetrate. Even if a scammer try's to pull the cable company scam, the operator will ask anyone trying to access the account for the password (even another operator). Most banks that use passwords, the password must be entered into the system before allowing access to any account or the account will not open. Plus, if the scammer say's they forgot the password, the company would most likely call the number listed on file to change and verify the caller. This will give you a 75% more chance of not only protecting your SS#, but also your accounts.

TIP! ! ! When customers call a company requesting a password be placed on their account, The company usually asks the reason for the password, so they can place

a note on the account. That way, when a representative handle's your account, they will deal with the person on the phone with caution until every things verified.

From my experience, it's always a turnoff when tring to break an account with a password, and 75% of the time, a scammer will disconnect the call when asked for a password. If the company you deal with doesn't offer password protection and they have your SS#. Close your account and pick a different company.

TIP! ! ! NEVER carry your social security card with you, if you don't have to. And if you apply for a credit card in a retail store, be sure to type your SS# on a pad connected to a register. Never say it out loud or write it down on a piece of paper, and when you type it in, cover it with your hand as you would your pin number for your bankcard.

How many times have you written your ss# on a application form? Now answer yourself!

This is a grave mistake and sometimes it can't be done any other way. Imagine this, a doctor office gives you an application to gain your insurance information. You fill it out, answering questions like, SS#, DOB, day time phone number, full name, address and; etc. . . Now you fill this application out in 2001 and that same doctor office shuts down in 2020. Where does all those applications go? That's 19 years of applications, can imagine how much personal information that's saved in all that time? Stop counting! Now back to the real question, where does all those applications go? The answer is, a warehouse, a storage, a safe or even worse, left in the same building the doctor's office used to be. So before you fill out an application, remember this!

TIP! ! ! This includes hospitals and online applications. BEWARE of this! The hospital staff may not be the one looking for this information, but scammers look in places like this every day. What if the company you filled out an application with online gets hacked!

SECOND STEP TO SCAM PREVENTION

Public records always leads to the start of identity theft. it takes nothing to gain someone's name, DOB and location. Social media are one of the leading sources to identity theft, and it's not because this information show's on your Profile! It's because these same social media site's sell your personal information to third party companies who in turn sell it to those same company' s who offer background checks on anybody in the world. Where did you think their information came from. Yep, it's all legal! So next time you sign up on another website, read the terms and conditions, before clicking agree. You'll most likely delete all your social media accounts.

Your credit report includes detailed personal information, Such as your full name, DOB, current and previous addresses, employment info and yep, you guess it, your SS#. Your public records are also listed.

TIP! ! ! Remember, sometimes there is incorrect information listed. This could be either a mistake or identity theft, so either way, you should file a dispute with the appropriate credit bureau to have the record corrected.

You will also find a section in your credit report that list any bankruptcies, liens, foreclosures or court rulings.

Even if the public records are accurate, you should verify the dates. By law, Negative information in your report, must be deleted after a specific period of time. If the allotted time period has passed, you can file a dispute and the information will be immediately removed from your report.

It seems like protecting your personal information is an all day job, and you should understand something. As humans we need our health to enjoy life, so look at it this way. Our health is similar to our personal information, because who wants to lose something they have built for many years.

TRACK1, TRACK 2!

Track 1 is the first set of numbers shown on your card, this is the 15 or 16 digit numbers on your card. Track 2 is the numbers on the black strip of your card, located on the back of your card. Track1, Track 2 is a term used by scammers . Usually a black box is involved, blank cards, a tipper and your card information. The scammer would

gain card numbers, but guess from where? If you guess your credit report, you are almost ready to prevent scam.

Credit reports show your account numbers, and get this, one credit report will show the first set of your account numbers, and another would show the last set of numbers (each credit beau shows the account numbers different) . Do i have to tell you that a scammer can uptain your whole account number this way. Now a scammer can only "PUNCH IN" with this type of information. Meaning, when a scammer makes a duplicate card using your account number, instead of swiping the card, the scammer would use it at any retail store and when the store clerk try's to swipe the card, an error will show up. The scammer would tell the store the card is damage, getting the clerk to type in (PUNCH IN) the card number instead. The reason the card can only PUNCH IN, is because in order to swipe a card, it must also have the track2 numbers, which can only be done using a black box card reading machine. Track1 is known to go be used by beginner and mid-level scammers. Pro scammers would use both track1 and track2 together.

TRACK1, TRACK 2 EXAMPLE

Anthony and Jack both worked at a restaurant and processed orders. One day, Anthony came up with a plan for some fast money. When customers give their cards to them, they would swipe the card on the restaurant's black box machine and their personal pocket black box machine that they bought from a Local electronic store. By doing this, they would gain all the cards information. After gaining the card info, Anthony and Jack take their personal black box home, using blank cards to duplicate the original card.

Tipping is a term used by scammers, who use a card dressing machine to put the name, card number, cvv, expiration date and color to the blank card, making the card seem legit. Once all this is done, Anthony and Jack can go to any company store or online and make purchases. You won't know about the purchases until after your account is maxed out. So how can you prevent this scam?

Follow this book and if you can, use your major credit cards and debit cards with companies that not only allow you to swipe your own card, but offer customer protection as well. And for meaningless purchases, use a prepaid card or secured card.

3 QUICK WAYS TO PREVENT SCAM! ! !

ONLINE:

Cyber criminals inundate shoppers with pop-up ads and emails linked to fake sites. So you think you're shopping at a real store, but your credit information is sent to scammers. To stay safe, shop at reputable site's that begin with "HTTPS" (meaning secure) Not "HTTP" and have a "LOCK" icon in the web address bar.

TIP! ! !

NEVER store (save) your address or card information on any website, Just in case it gets hacked. Instead, check out as a "GUESS"

DEVICE!!!

Shopping on your tablet or phone while you wait in a coffee shop may be efficient, but if you use public WI-FI, snoopers can steal data over open air waves. That's why it's best to use a virtual private network (VPN) to securely encrypt connections in public. You can download the software to your phone.

STORE!!!

In this new scamming, generation of pick pocket. A scammer can steal without even touching you, using sensors that retrieve the radio frequency identification (RFID), technology that's embedded in many credit cards. Your information can be stolen out of thin air. It's best to use cards that offer RFID protection.

TIP!!!

If a store clerk asks for your birthday, phone number, zip code or SS#. Don't give it! It takes nothing to steal someone's identity.

YOU CAN PREVENT SCAM!!!

Remember, we went through how most information can be stolen from your doctors' office and hospitals. Protect your insurance card as fiercely as a credit card! If you lose it, tell your insurer immediately. And read medical bills carefully, it's easy to overlook fraudulent expenses.

Also, protect your email address! Many email providers now offer two factor authentication, where you can't log in until you enter a temporary code that's sent via text to your cell phone number. This option can be found in "account settings" This alert is similar to the credit report alert system we mention earlier.

There is no one way to prevent scam, but the only way to combat it, is to learn from those who did it. The realty of things is that there will always be a new way to scam and get around systems to help prevent scam. Remember,

the plan is to make it hard for someone to gain access to your information, discouraging the scammer.

TIP! ! !

If you receive an official looking Letter from Medicare or social security administration (SSA) asking you to call, DON'T CALL! Dial the trusted numbers (800-663-4277) for medical and 800-772-1213 for SSA.

More information will be given in my next book, PRO SCAMMER!

TIP ! ! !

The three major credit bureaus (Equifax, Experian and TransUnion) offer alerts when someone try's to open a new account in your name. And, before an account is open with your SS#, an alert will come via phone. The creditor will notice the alert on your credit report, along with the phone number you placed with the alert. A call will be placed to you, asking "Are you the one trying to open said account."

ABOUT THE AUTHOR

D. MORGAN is the author of The New World Banking System novel, has mastered the techniques of scamming and identity theft. He is a motivational speaker and founder of Each One Reach One foundation which is a non-profit organization. Having served a 6-year sentence for identify theft and fraud, he has turned his life around. Now helping people who are affected by identity thief.

Books coming soon by D. Morgan:

Pro Scammer

Company Fraud

Statistics

New World Banking system Part 2

Printed in the United States
By Bookmasters